The Herself the Elf Storybook

SCHOLASTIC INC.
New York Toronto London Auckland Sydney Tokyo

ISBN 0-590-32911-1

12 11 10 9 8 7 6 5 4 3 2   3 4 5 6 7/8
Printed in the U.S.A.   10

Storybook Adapted by Lisa Norby
from the teleplay by Dianne Dixon

Artwork prepared by
Nelvana Limited, Toronto, Canada,
for the "Herself the Elf" television special.

Design by Russell D'Anna/Diane Addesso

It was a lovely afternoon in the forest.
The sun was shining brightly. The birds were singing.
And in the clearing by the old oak tree, Herself the Elf
was teaching a baby fawn to walk.

"Are you ready?" she asked. "It's time for you to take
your first steps."

The fawn whinnied softly and pulled himself up on
his long, spindly legs.

"Good for you!" said Herself. "I knew you could do
it."

The fawn's legs were still very unsteady. But every time he stumbled, Herself waved her magic wand and pulled him to his feet.

Soon all the creatures of the forest had gathered to watch Herself the Elf at work. "Isn't it wonderful," they whispered to each other, "how Herself keeps nature running so smoothly! Everything is just the way it was when her father, the old Elf King, was alive."

Sometimes, though, Herself the Elf wondered how she could possibly get all her day's work done. Taking over her father's job as ruler of the elf kingdom had not been easy. All of nature was depending on her. She had to make sure the sun woke up on time, that the flowers had their morning dew to drink, and that the birds had their singing lessons...

Now she turned to her friends and said, "I promise that I will do my very best to make every day beautiful."

"Your best won't be good enough, dearie," cackled a voice high up in the tallest tree. Unknown to the group in the clearing, Vendetta the vulture was spying on them. As soon as she had seen her fill, Vendetta flapped her wings menacingly and took off to report to her boss, the evil Thorn.

In his castle, inside the hollow tree that stands in the middle of the swamp, Thorn was hard at work. For every magic spell Herself knew to make nature run smoothly, Thorn had a recipe for trouble. At the moment, he was in his laboratory, mixing up a batch of itchy, scratchy weeds.

"AH-CHOO—AH-CHOOO!" Thorn sneezed as he worked. "All this sunlight is making my allergies act up," he wheezed. "I can't wait till I find a way to take over Herself's magic powers. When I do, I'll make things nice and gloomy, just the way I like them."

Just then, Vendetta flew in. "Herself is in the clearing now, master," she croaked. "If we kidnap her right away, we'll be sure to get her magic wand too."

"That's it!" Thorn jumped up and down in glee. "As soon as I control that wand, nature will be *my* domain...all mine! First, I'll make the robins caw like crows. Then I'll turn all the flowers gray..."

"And then, you'll make me queen!" chimed in Thorn's daughter, Creeping Ivy. "Won't you, Daddy? Please?"

"Not unless you prove yourself worthy," snorted Thorn. "And even then, I might only make you Ambassador of Gloom."

Creeping Ivy shrugged and turned back to her mirror to adjust her new spider earrings. "I can live with that," she said, reaching out to grab one of the spiders as it tried to crawl away.

"Now," muttered Thorn, pacing up and down, "all I have to do is figure out a way to get Herself and the magic wand."

"I can do that, Daddy," said Creeping Ivy. With a snap of her fingers, she sent one of her tendrils whipping across the room.

"Now!" she commanded. "Go find Herself the Elf and dump her in Daddy's enchanted garden."

All at once, the tendril began to grow. It snaked out the door of Thorn's castle and down the trunk of the old hollow tree.

It leaped over the waters of the swamp, and it slithered across the floor of the forest, all the way to the clearing where Herself and her friends were playing.

Before anyone noticed, the tendril crept up behind the fawn and wrapped itself around his legs. Then it caught a little white rabbit. Both animals squealed in terror.

"Don't be afraid! I'll save you," Herself cried. And she wrestled with the slithery arms of the vine. First the fawn wriggled out of the tendril's viselike grasp. Then the rabbit popped free too. Herself was not so lucky. As she struggled with the vine, her wand slipped out of her hand and fell to the ground with a sad little tinkling sound. At that moment, Herself the Elf lost all her magic powers.

"Run! Hurry up! Save yourselves and warn the other elves," Herself shouted as the vine tightened its grip and dragged her away.

This was just the moment Vendetta had been waiting for. In a flash, she swooped down, grabbed the wand in her beak, and carried it off to Thorn's castle.

"Hooray! My plan worked," Thorn cackled when he finally held the magic wand in his very own bony hands.

"*Your* plan?" whined Creeping Ivy. "I did all the work. Now how about my reward?"

"Not so fast," said Thorn. "Legend says that when the magic wand is parted from its true owner, it will lose its power for a year and a day. Patience, my dear. In good time, *we* will be rulers of the forest."

For a whole year Herself the Elf was held prisoner in Thorn's enchanted garden. It was the saddest place she had ever seen. Stinging nettles grew all over the ground, and the walls were covered with bramble vines. Every day was dark and dreary. The future looked dim indeed.

But Herself did not give up hope. For a whole year and most of the last day, she kept searching for a way to escape. "Only six hours left. I must find a way to get my wand," Herself vowed as she tried again to climb up over the bramble-covered walls.

At that very moment, although Herself did not know it, four very tired elves were making their way along a path in the forest.

"Time is running out," said the first elf sadly. "We've been searching for Herself for a whole year, and we've had no luck at all."

"I know," agreed the second elf. "Maybe we should give up."

"We can't stop," scolded the third elf. "We've got to rescue Herself from Thorn's evil clutches."

The fourth elf was lagging behind the rest. As she strolled along, she was making up a little tune inside her head. "Oh, dear," she said when she reached a fork in the path. "Which way did they go?

"Did they go this way? Or that way?" She was so confused that she ran around in circles and made herself dizzy.

Frantically, she chose a path and—*whomp!*—ran right into someone she had never seen before.

"Who...who are you?" asked the fourth little elf, when she had picked herself up.

"I'm Wilfie the wood sprite," said the stranger. "We are distant cousins of the elves. But who are you? And what's the big rush?"

"I am Willow Song," the little elf said. "I'm looking for my friends, but I don't know where they went. Our leader, Herself the Elf, has been kidnapped by Thorn, and we must rescue her."

"So Thorn's up to his old tricks," said Wilfie. "I was his prisoner not long ago, and I was lucky to escape with my life. If there's anything I can do, I'll be glad to help you."

"That's wonderful," said Willow Song. "The first thing you can do is help me find the other elves."

"No problem," answered Wilfie. "Sprites are expert pathfinders. Just follow me!"

The two friends soon caught up with the others.

"This is Wilfie," said Willow Song. "He's volunteered to help us."

"Good," said Elf number one. "Then we should introduce ourselves properly. I am Meadow Morn, elf in charge of the animal kingdom."

"I am Woodpink," said Elf number two. "I am responsible for all the colors in nature." Woodpink, who could not resist showing off, waved her wand and changed the wildflowers and the leaves into all the colors of the rainbow and back again to the way they were.

"I am Snowdrop," said the third elf. "I take care of the water and air." Snowdrop gave her wand a little shake and produced a fluffy white cloud that slowly floated up into the sky.

"Ahem!" Meadow Morn cleared her throat and glared in the direction of Willow Song.

"Oh...oh, yes," said Willow Song. "I am in charge of all the sounds in nature. In fact, I hear a very unusual sound right this minute!"

"You do!" exclaimed the other elves. "What is it?"

"Maybe..." said Willow Song. "Maybe..."

"A Maybe! What's a Maybe?" asked Snowdrop.

"No, no, no...I mean *maybe* it's Herself," answered Willow Song happily. "It *is* Herself. I'm sure of it now!"

Willow Song ran off in the direction of Herself's voice. Fortunately, she was much better at following sounds than at following directions, and she led Wilfie and the other elves straight to the hidden entrance to Thorn's enchanted garden!

"Now how do we get inside?" asked Meadow Morn as she tugged uselessly at the bramble-covered garden gate. "It won't budge."

"I can help with that," Wilfie said. He pointed to a weird-looking clump of brambles that seemed to be growing right out of the center of the gate. "That's Thorn's secret latch. I saw one just like it when I was a prisoner in his castle."

Wilfie grabbed five long twigs that were shaped just like bony fingers and pulled them three times. Sure enough, the gate swung open with a loud creak.

"Hooray! Hooray!" shouted Herself as the other elves rushed into the garden. "You've rescued me! And just in time too!"

"What a hideous place!" exclaimed Woodpink, looking around at the clumps of choking weeds and droopy flowers. "Why didn't you use your wand to neaten things up?"

"Vendetta took my magic wand away," Herself said. "It is hidden in Thorn's castle. I must get it back before midnight or all my elf powers will pass into Thorn's control. And your powers, too, for that matter, since you are my assistants."

"How awful!" the elves agreed. "We'll find it for you! Let's hurry!" And all four elves rushed out of the garden at once, tripping over each other's feet in their haste.

"Oh, dear," sighed Herself. "They mean well, but they're so disorganized." Then, for the first time, she noticed Wilfie. He had been standing quietly just inside the gate. "But who are you?" she asked.

"I'm Wilfie the wood sprite. Maybe I can help."

"Good," said Herself. "It looks as if I'll need all the help I can get. Let's hurry and try to catch up with the others."

The four elves were already at the entrance
to the swamp.

"How will we ever get across all this water?" Woodpink sniffed. "It's awfully dirty and smelly."

"And dangerous too!" gasped Willow Song.

"Let's split up," said Meadow Morn. "And each of us
will look for a way to get across."

After the others had gone, Meadow Morn had a good
idea. She would get the animals to help her!

Sweeping her wand back and forth,
she sang:

Beavers near and far,
From every lake and stream and pond,
Answer now the summons of my wand!

Pop...pop...pop... Dozens of beavers popped their heads out of the water and swam to Meadow Morn's side. Soon they were hard at work, building a log bridge across the swamp, right up to the castle door.

In the meantime, Woodpink was searching through the dark underbrush nearby. Suddenly a big, ugly spider dropped down, landing right on her beautiful hair.

"*Yeech!*" she screamed. "That does it! I'm going to turn all these creepy crawly creatures white. That way I'll see them before they have a chance to scare me."

Woodpink waved her wand and chanted:

Insects and animals here around,
I now make you white as the snow on the ground.

Her spell worked all too well. The beavers had just finished the bridge, when suddenly they were turned white as snow! "What's going on here!" chattered the frightened beavers.

Unfortunately, just at that moment, Vendetta flew overhead. She made one low pass over Meadow Morn and the beavers, and then she turned toward the castle.

"Help! Snowdrop! Woodpink! Willow Song! Come here!" shouted Meadow Morn. "We've got to stop Vendetta."

All the elves came running.

"Don't worry. I'll fix everything," cried Snowdrop. She waved her magic wand and chanted:

Rain and thunder, hear my call,
Stop this vulture once and for all.

A torrent of water poured from the sky, and a wicked-looking bolt of lightning crackled overhead. Vendetta managed to dart out of its way in time.

But the beavers' bridge was swept away on the rising tide of the storm.

"All is not yet lost," cried Willow Song, arriving last as usual. "I'll make sure Vendetta will never be able to tell what she knows." And she pointed her wand in the air and cried:

You at whom I point my wand,
Sing us all a bluebird's song.

But before Willow Song could get the words out, she tripped over a rock and her wand pointed at the beavers instead of Vendetta. In a flash, the beavers began to sing like bluebirds.

"What a mess you've all made!" said Meadow Morn.

"We were just trying to help," wailed the others.

They were sitting dejectedly beside the ruined bridge when Herself and Wilfie arrived. "This will teach us to work together next time," Herself the Elf scolded. "We've got to learn to cooperate."

"That's right," said Wilfie. "If you hadn't been in such a hurry I would have had time to tell you that I know a secret entrance to Thorn's castle. Come along."

The elves stopped just long enough to change the beavers back to normal. Then everyone marched off with Wilfie in the lead.

One by one they went down into the secret entrance. In no time, they were inside the castle. They all stayed close together as they tiptoed down the damp, musty corridor that led to Thorn's laboratory ...all, that is, except Woodpink, who stopped for just a second to check her hairdo in one of the big oval mirrors that lined the walls.

As Woodpink peered into the mirror, a huge spider detached itself from the frame and scuttled up her arm. "*Yikes!* It's alive!" she shrieked, and ran as fast as her feet would carry her, trying to shake off the spider as she went.

When Woodpink stopped running, she was alone in a distant part of the castle. "Oh, dear," she murmured. "I'll never find the others now. Someone is coming! I'd better hide."

She checked all the doors along the hallway until she found a coal bin. That looked like just the place! Then, with a flick of her wand, she drained all the color from her face and hair and made herself look just like the coal in the bin.

Not a minute later, the door creaked open, and Creeping Ivy's voice pierced the darkness. "What's going on? I know that silly elf is in here."

Closer and closer came Creeping Ivy until she was right in front of Woodpink. "Ah ha! Lookie what I found!" she chuckled.

Sure enough, the color had slowly begun to return to Woodpink's face. As Creeping Ivy dragged her away, Woodpink stared at her magic wand in astonishment. Something was terribly wrong. Her wand's power seemed to be draining away...and just when she needed it most!

By now, the others had reached the door to Thorn's laboratory. "We'll have to climb up this vine that leads to the open transom," said Wilfie.

"But I...I...I'll never make it," squealed Willow Song. "I'm terribly afraid of high places."

"Very well," answered Herself. "Then you go back and look for Woodpink. I don't know where she wandered off to!"

As Herself and Wilfie pulled themselves up the vine, a dark shadow swooped into the hall behind them. It was Vendetta!

"Don't worry," shouted Snowdrop from below. "I'll stop her." And she waved her wand and chanted:

To save the elves and Wilfie the sprite,
Stir up a wind to blow with all its might!

WHOOOSH!!! In answer to Snowdrop's call, a big wind blew up and sent Vendetta reeling.

Herself and Wilfie leaped to safety on the other side of the big door. But before Snowdrop and Meadow Morn could follow, the wind puffed and poofed and died down all together.

"Oh, no!" cried Meadow Morn. "It must be almost twelve o'clock. Our magic wands are losing their power." She and Snowdrop huddled against the door. "We're sure to be caught now," she said.

Inside Thorn's lab, Herself and Wilfie were making their way through a forest of giant test tubes. "I know my wand must be hidden in here," Herself whispered. "We've got to find it and save our friends...and all of nature too."

Suddenly, a huge glass jar swung down out of nowhere. Wilfie was trapped! "Now I've got you!" cackled Creeping Ivy. "And as for you, my little friend," she added, snaking out a tendril in Herself's direction, "you are hissss...tory!"

"You haven't got us yet," said Herself. She jumped away and ran into the dark recesses of the laboratory, where there were a lot of good hiding places.

Wilfie knew some tricks too.

At the little sprite's command, his caterpillar hat slithered out of the opening in the jar. *Smack!* It kissed Creeping Ivy's hand. *"EEEEK!!!"* screamed Creeping Ivy. *"Yuck! Icky!* Get away from me!" And she dropped the jar.

Wilfie was free. But Herself was not. Creeping Ivy had found her and trapped her at the edge of a nasty-looking chasm.

"This time I've got you for sure," hissed Creeping Ivy as Herself inched her way backward along a narrow plank. Raising her arms, Creeping Ivy sent a hundred snaky tendrils toward her prey.

Herself grabbed one of the tendrils and swung up and down on the plank, sending Creeping Ivy tumbling into the chasm.

"It'll take her a while to climb out of there," Herself said, peering into the darkness. "Let's find my wand."

Herself pointed to a scraggly heap of twigs perched up on a high ledge. "Look," she said to Wilfie. "I'll bet that's where the wand is hidden. In Vendetta's nest!"

Wilfie boosted Herself up onto his shoulders, and she reached into the mass of twigs. "It's here," she cried. "I've almost got it!"

"Almost isn't good enough, my dear. Look at the clock. It's one minute to twelve," cried Thorn as he swept into the room with the smirking Vendetta perched on his shoulder. "Seize them!" he commanded, and Vendetta rose into the air, heading straight for Wilfie and Herself.

Vendetta would have made short work of the one small elf and a wood sprite if Willow Song hadn't happened to wander through the open door of the lab.

"Oh, oh," gasped Willow Song. "I hope there's one more spell left in my wand." Shaking it hard, she chanted:

To save us all quick as can be,
Give the voice of Thorn to...ME!!!

It worked! Thorn's big commanding voice boomed out of Willow Song's mouth. "Vendetta!" it called. "Come here this instant."

The bewildered vulture wheeled around in mid-flight and crashed right into Thorn.

Thorn shook himself free from Vendetta and made one last desperate lunge toward Herself.

But one of Creeping Ivy's tendrils had slithered in through the door and was tugging at his robe. "Daddy! Daddy! Look what I caught!" squealed Creeping Ivy as she entered the lab. She was carrying Woodpink, Meadow Morn, and Snowdrop in a big wooden cage.

"Not now, daughter," wheezed Thorn. "Can't you see this isn't the time for that. Let me go!"

It was too late. In the confusion, Herself's fingers closed around the magic wand. As the clock struck midnight, she could feel her powers flowing back.

"I've got it!" she cried. "We've won! Nature is saved from Thorn's wicked scheme!"

In a flash, Herself waved the wand and set Woodpink, Meadow Morn, and Snowdrop free. Then all the elves touched wands to make their magic strong again.

"Now we can do a little house-cleaning around here," said Meadow Morn. Waving her wand in the direction of the screeching, howling Vendetta, she commanded:

The time has come to end our fears,

Let Vendetta sleep for a thousand years.

Immediately Vendetta dropped onto a cobwebby sofa and began snoring loudly.

"Good for you!" laughed Snowdrop. "I think we could use some fresh air too." She shook her wand, and the shutters of the castle flew open, letting in a cool, fresh breeze.

"And some light too," added Woodpink, summoning a legion of fireflies in through the open windows.

"AH-CHOO! AH-CHOO!" sneezed Thorn. "This is awful. I'm *allergic* to light and fresh air."

"You can't *do* this to my daddy," screeched Creeping Ivy.

"Oh, yes, we can," said Herself. "And Willow Song has a special treat for you."

Ugly spiders on her ears, chanted Willow Song.
Fiddle a tune that will bring her to tears.

Immediately, Creeping Ivy's spider earrings started to dance and sing. "I hate music," she wailed. "It always makes me cry." Tears splattered down her cheeks, and everywhere they landed, Creeping Ivy sprouted a new tendril. The new sprouts grew so fast that soon Creeping Ivy was tied up in them.

And they kept on growing...until Vendetta and Thorn were tied up too.

The elves and Wilfie ran out of the castle and didn't stop running until they had reached the safety of the forest. Then, just for a moment, they looked back over the dark waters of the swamp to the hollow tree and Thorn's castle. What they saw made them gasp. The vines that had sprouted from Creeping Ivy's tears had sealed up the knothole doors and wrapped themselves tightly around the hollow tree's trunk and branches.

"It looks as if we will be safe from Thorn and Creeping Ivy for a long time to come," said Wilfie thoughtfully. "The forest creatures can live in peace from now on."

"Good. I'd better get back home," said Herself. "I have a lot of work to do."

"Work!" The other elves groaned.

Herself smiled. "All right. There will be plenty of time for that tomorrow. Today we'll have a party to celebrate our victory. The whole forest is invited, and our new friend Wilfie will be the guest of honor."

"Hooray! Hooray!" cried the elves and Wilfie too. And hand in hand, they all went back to Herself's little house in the clearing.